Contents

Paul Bunyan
Logging Legend

It's not clear where the first stories about Paul Bunyan came from. Some think he was invented by loggers sitting around campfires in the late 1800s. Others claim he was the creation of a Detroit newspaperman who published a famous story about Paul called "The Round-River Drive" in 1910. No matter where the tales of Paul Bunyan were "born," it's clear that he is one of the best-known characters in some of America's tallest tall tales.

PAUL BUNYAN was the best and smartest logger in history. So it's no surprise that lots of towns and states like to say he was born within their borders. Most folks believe he was born in the great state of Maine. Others say Minnesota. But since Paul was so big — even as a newborn baby — he could have been born in more than one state at once.

Paul grew fast — probably because he ate so much. For breakfast he'd gobble down three pots of oatmeal mush, four dozen eggs, and five gallons of milk. That was nothing compared to what he ate for lunch and dinner.

By the time he was three weeks old, Paul's size began to cause some problems. Seems he turned over in his cradle and accidentally knocked down about four miles of tall trees. The townspeople, of course, were upset. They told Paul's parents that they would have to keep him somewhere where he wouldn't do so much damage.

Paul's father was an ordinary-sized man, and he had a knack for building things. So he used the timber from the trees Paul had knocked over to build a giant cradle. Then he and Paul's mama set the cradle to drift at sea with a five-hundred-foot rope.

Paul seemed happy enough out at sea in his cradle. He liked to watch the sun and the sky and the clouds and the birds. One day, he saw a whole flock of geese. Excited, he waved his arms and kicked his legs, as most babies will do. Except that Paul was about fifty times bigger than most babies. He rocked his cradle so hard it caused tidal waves. Villages all up and down the coast were flooded.

Now the people were really mad, and they stormed up to Paul's house.

"Your baby is nothing but trouble!" they shouted. "Get him out of here before he drowns the whole state!"

Of course, Paul's parents felt bad. They were good folks and didn't want to cause any problems. So they quietly packed up their belongings and Paul and moved away. But deep down they were secretly proud of their strapping baby boy.

Nobody knows for sure where Paul and his family went. Some say they headed deep into the woods, where Paul caused more than one earthquake when he was learning to crawl. Others say they climbed high into the mountains, where Paul created several avalanches when he took his first steps. It wasn't until Paul became a full-sized man that folks discovered his whereabouts once again.

Paul had grown so big that folks in Ohio could see the top of his curly black head as soon as he set foot on the eastern side of Pennsylvania. He stood more than fifty feet tall, and his feet were the size of school buses. Paul's dark eyes were as big as serving platters, his nose like a giant leg of lamb. His bristly black beard (which some swear he was born with) was so long and so thick that he used a dozen ten-foot pine boughs just to comb it in the morning.

Then there was his clothes. It took an entire year's crop of cotton just to make enough cloth for his pants and shirt. His suspenders were made from three-foot-wide rope. And making his boots used up all the leather in Maine, Pennsylvania, and Ohio put together.

Having been raised in the wild, Paul was naturally drawn to the giant forests that covered America. Back then, when the country was fresh and pure, it was covered with trees. And not like the trees of today. These trees grew so tall and so thick that if you stood in the middle of a forest and looked up, you could barely see the sky. America was still brand new, and folks hadn't taken down forests yet to build houses and churches and general stores.

One day, Paul was taking his morning romp through the woods. As he combed his bushy black beard with a giant pine bough, he came up with an idea. "Why, I think I'll become a lumberjack," he told the forest animals. "I'll cut down some of America's trees so folks can build themselves towns to live in."

Paul began to chop down trees — he called it logging — and discovered that he was mighty good at it. What's more, he loved it. He loved the crisp forest air. He loved the smell of pine boughs and fresh sap. And he loved the weight of the ax in his hands.

In just a few short weeks, Paul had logged his way across the state of Maine and was getting ready to move on down to New Hampshire and Vermont. But as much as he loved logging, Paul was feeling a little lonely.

"Life and logging would be better," he told himself, "if I had someone to share them with."

Paul didn't have to wait too long to find

a friend. Because not long after that came the Winter of the Blue Snow. Now, lots of strange things happened back in Paul Bunyan's day. But the Winter of the Blue Snow was one of the strangest. As Paul strode through the woods one day, being careful not to knock over any trees or start any landslides, he marveled at the giant blue snowflakes that fell from the sky.

"They're beautiful!" Paul exclaimed, catching a few thousand snowflakes on his tongue. He was about to catch another drift of snow when he heard pitiful crying. Turning on his heel (and nearly crushing a giant boulder under his foot), Paul headed off toward the noise.

Soon Paul came to a small blue mountain. It was strange, but the mountain seemed to be making a whimpering sound. It was so loud Paul wanted to cover his ears. But he had some investigating to do.

"Now, I've seen almost everything in these woods, but I've never known a mountain to whimper," he said to himself. "Then again, I've never seen a *blue* mountain, either."

Just then, Paul noticed two white tree trunks that were sticking out of the mountain's sides. He grabbed hold of those tree trunks and pulled.

Lo and behold, the mountain wasn't a mountain at all. It was a baby ox! The ox was as blue as the snow, and just as frozen. He stared at Paul with wide eyes, then whimpered some more.

Paul picked up that baby blue ox and carried him home. He wrapped him in blankets and held him on his lap, snuggling him close in front of a roaring fire all night long. The ox was still as anything, and Paul hoped he would be okay.

The next morning, Paul awoke to the strangest sensation he'd ever felt. Some-

thing big, wet, and rough was wrapping itself around his neck! Paul's neck was his
only ticklish spot, and he laughed so hard
the walls of his house fell down, and
plenty of trees outside, too.

"Stop that!" he roared with a belly
laugh. Paul looked up to see the baby blue
ox, who was furiously kissing his neck. The
ox stepped back, knocking over all of
Paul's furniture. He looked at his new
papa with giant black eyes.

Paul grinned, for he knew his lonely
days were over. He'd found a friend. "I'm
going to call you Babe," he declared. "And
together we're going to log the North
Country so people can have lumber to
build with."

After that, Paul and Babe were always
together. Paul fed Babe soup and love,
and soon he was a full-grown giant ox. Nobody knows exactly how giant. But many
say he measured more than forty-two ax

handles between the eyes. And his hoof-prints were big enough to create the thousands of lakes found in the northern states.

Together Paul and Babe logged their way across the northern part of America, all the way to Michigan, Wisconsin, and Minnesota. Babe was a huge help to Paul but also full of mischief. He liked to play tricks and wander off. But since you couldn't see all the way across one of his hoofprints on a foggy morning, he was awfully hard to track. Paul spent many a day and night looking for his not-so-trusty companion and was always greeted with a rough tongue tickle when he finally found him.

By the time Paul and Babe got to the North Woods of the Midwest, Paul was interested in finding more friends. "You're a heck of a companion," he told Babe. "But I think I'd like to have some other lumberjacks to talk to."

So Paul built a logging camp and hired some men to work for him.

Paul Bunyan had two requirements for his men. They had to be big, and they had to be strong. Not one of the men in his camp was shorter than seven feet or weighed less than three hundred pounds.

There was Big Swede Ole, the best and fastest blacksmith ever. He could shoe four horses at once, holding them all in his lap like little babies. There was Joe Inkslinger, Paul's bookkeeper. Joe worked the books so fast and furious that they had to store his extra ink in Lake Superior to keep from running out. And there was Brimstone Bill, who took care of the animals. Bill could milk a dozen cows at once with his left hand while collecting eggs from the hens with his right.

Not to mention the loggers themselves. Nobody knew exactly how many men Paul had in his camp, because they were always coming and going, busy with work. But three thousand sounds like a pretty good guess.

It might sound impossible to house so many men. But Paul was clever. He built stackable bunkhouses and piled them one on top of the other. "Now I just need some mighty tall, straight trees," he said. It didn't take Paul long to find some, and he used them to build a kind of monorail track up the sides. The men rode down in the mornings and up in the evenings.

To keep his three thousand men fed, Paul hired the best cooks he could find. There was Sourdough Sam, Hot Biscuit Slim, Big Joe Muffington, and Hotcake Hankie, to name a few. They all got to work twenty-eight hours before daylight so they could keep those hungry loggers fed.

And who could forget the cookees, who were in charge of getting the hot food to the men. This job wasn't easy, because the dining halls were so long it took nearly a

week to get from one end to another —
and that was on roller skates (which Paul
himself invented).

Paul's cooks used Minnesota's famous
lakes, which Babe created with his giant
hooves, as mixing bowls. They stirred up
biscuit dough with spoons carved from giant white pine trees. The hotcake batter
took a little more creativity. After filling a
good-sized lake with the ingredients, Paul
set an actual steamboat paddling across
it — back and forth, back and forth. In
just a couple of days, the batter was mixed
and ready for the griddle.

Then there was the split-pea stockpot.
Paul chose a nice deep lake and dug a giant trench all the way around it. His men
built roaring fires in the trench so they
could use the lake to simmer Sourdough
Sam's famous split-pea soup. The soup
lake needed so much heat that three
bunkhouses of cookees carried wood

around the clock to keep the fires burning.

No matter what the food, the ration was always the same. Half of the food was for the three thousand lumberjacks, and the other half was split between Paul and Babe.

Of all the delicious soups, stews, and other dishes that Paul's cooks turned out, their favorite was hotcakes — steaming hotcakes smothered in wagonloads of butter and maple syrup. The problem was, Ole could not seem to make a griddle big enough to keep those hotcakes coming.

So Paul got to thinking.

"Come on, Babe," he said. "You and I are taking a little trip." The two set off for the ironworks a few states away. He had those ironworkers build him the biggest round hotcake griddle this country has ever seen.

When the griddle was ready, Paul

hitched it to Babe and had the big blue ox pull it to the top of a mountain. Then Paul let the griddle go, and it rolled and rolled for miles, right into his camp. When it got to the best spot, that griddle spun around and around, settling down in the dust. All that spinning dug a giant hole underneath it. That hole was a good thing, since you practically needed a forest fire to keep the griddle hot.

Paul's new griddle was so big it took three men just to see from one side to the other. To keep it greased up, Paul had a hundred of his bravest cookees strap hunks of bacon fat to their feet and skate across it. Then the batter was poured in circles the size of wagon wheels onto the griddle through a giant, hollowed-out pine tree. Before long, the whole camp was chowing down on Hotcake Hankie's biggest, best hotcakes.

Those hotcakes — along with the other delectables — kept Paul's men fed and happy. They worked hard that winter and logged so many trees that soon there were mountains of lumber all over the state. Sometimes it took the loggers so long to get over the lumber mountains they had built that they had to start back to camp as soon as they got to the other side.

"We've got to get rid of these logs," Paul declared one morning. The problem was, the road nearby was so crooked that it kept forgetting which way it was going. Some folks say it spelled out all the letters of the alphabet — twice! There was no way to get the logs down that road without cutting them into corkscrews. They needed a road that went in a nice straight line.

Then one day, Paul got an idea. He fed Babe an extra two tons of hotcakes and hitched him up to one end of the road.

"You can do it, Babe," he whispered, giving the ox several pats on the back.

Babe looked at Paul and looked back at

the road. He braced himself and hunkered down so low his belly almost touched the ground. The muscles on his back tensed so tight they looked like rocky peaks.

Babe inched forward. At first the road didn't move. Then, little by little, it began to straighten out. The loggers cheered, and Babe kept pulling.

It took all day, but Babe the Blue Ox straightened out that road. Once it had been pulled into a straight line, there were several hundred miles of road left over. Not wanting to waste anything, Paul put that road down somewhere else where there hadn't been a road before. Today that new road is called Interstate 80.

Now that the logging road was straight, Paul and his men had no trouble getting the logs to the mills. The trees that they cut helped people all over the country build homes, churches, schools, and stores.

Paul, his men, and Babe logged for many years. But, eventually, Paul began to miss some of the trees that he'd cut down. He thought it might be a good idea to let the trees grow back. By then he was getting on in years, and so was Babe. He'd logged clear across America. Some say he logged up into the Arctic Circle as well.

"I think it's time we find something else to do," Paul told Babe one fine fall evening as they gazed at the stars.

Babe made a grunting sound and nuzzled Paul's neck in response.

So Paul packed up his few belongings and headed off somewhere — nobody is quite sure where. But if you listen real close as you're strolling through the great American woods, you just might hear the echo of Paul Bunyan's voice calling, "T-I-M-B-E-R."

Sal Fink
Roaring River Gal

Sal Fink was the daughter of Mink Fink, the rudest and rowdiest keelboatman on the Mississippi in the late 1700s. Sal had her father's strength and courage but was not the bully he was known to be.

Sal Fink became famous when exaggerated stories about her (and her parents) appeared in newspapers and magazines in the early 1800s. Today she is one of America's most popular female tall-tale heroes.

SAL FINK was the roughest, toughest gal on the Mississippi River. Folks claim that she had rough blood running through her veins on account of her father being Mink Fink, the wildest keelboatman on the Mississippi River. Her mama wasn't someone to mess with, either. The very day little Sal was born, Sal's mama fought off a family of wildcats with her bare hands.

The folks along the river called Sal the Mississippi Screamer, on account of the way she howled whenever she was in a mood. They say Sal was in a mood the day she was born. Seems she got upset when she saw those wildcats pestering her mama. She opened her mouth and let loose a scream so loud it shook the houses for three miles up and down the river. It helped scare off the varmints, too.

Just like her parents, Sal could be as gentle as a spring breeze or as tough as a grizzly bear. It just depended on how she was feeling.

By the time Sal was five, she was see-sawing with alligators on the giant crags in the Mississippi River. One time, an alligator got so feisty that it chomped off its half of the log.

"Hi-ii-yo!" Sal hollered. She leaped onto the writhing gator's back and rode him like a bucking bronco until the poor creature was plumb tuckered out.

After that, the gator usually played fair when Sal was around. Whenever it didn't, Sal would hop right on its back and ride him up and down the river like a pony. She always belted "Yankee Doodle" at the top of her lungs as she rode and waved to the folks on the steamboats when she passed them by.

One time, little Sal was out rompin' in the woods when she came across a pair of panther cubs. They were cute as anything, and the three took up a game of chase.

The next thing Sal knew, the panthers' mama came flying out of a nearby tree, landing square on her back.

It was quite a tussle, since the panther had surprise on her side. *And* she was mad. Screeching loud as anything, that beast sunk her sharp claws into Sal's shoulder.

That did it. Sal was not about to be out-screeched by a panther. And she *always* liked to be in charge.

"Yeeeeeeee-owwww-owwww-owwww!" Sal screeched back.

The panther was so shocked that she froze, staring at Sal with her yellow eyes. Then she slinked back up the tree.

After that, Sal decided it was time to head home. The game of chase was over. But she hadn't gone fifty miles when she realized that the two panther cubs were following her. Seems Sal's screech was so powerful and pantherlike, they wanted her to be their new mama. Sal had no choice but to take the cubs in and care for them as best she could.

Taking care of those panther cubs was hard work. They were still babies, and needed someone to do most of their hunting. Luckily they weren't picky eaters.

One day, Sal decided they all could do with a delicious crawfish dinner. So she and the cubs set out to the river to catch some. Sal didn't use a net like most crawfisherfolks. Rather, she just snuck up on the critters and grabbed them with her bare hands. The cubs sat on the riverbank watching her for a while, then tried their own paws at crawfishing. They caught one crawfish apiece for every dozen of Sal's.

The cubs and Sal had just about filled a fifty-gallon bucket when a storm closed in. One minute the sky was so blue you could swim in it, and the next it was black as coal.

Before Sal could move her bucket away from the riverbank, the sky opened up and let loose. Rain poured down like Niagara Falls, and the river rose five feet in just under thirty seconds. Sal's crawfish were all washed away.

Sal shook her fist at the sky.

"I'm not lettin' a little weather get the best crawfish in these parts!" she shouted. Sal dove into the swirling mass of muddy water and rescued her crawfish from the hungry current.

Just then, a thunderbolt shot down out of the sky in a flash of blinding light. Quick as a wink, Sal grabbed ahold.

"Yipp-ee-ii-ii-oh!" she bellowed, wrestling that thunderbolt to the ground. Sparks flew everywhere, some clear back into the sky.

Soon that bolt of lightning was nothing more than a few zillion sparks flitting around on the ground. Sal picked them up in her skirt and carried them home. She carried the fifty-gallon bucket full of crawfish on her head.

When she got home, Sal wrapped those

sparks up nice and neat and tied the package off with string. She sent all those lightning sparks off to Uncle Sam's artillerymen, who used them to fire off their cannons.

That night, Sal, her mama and papa, and the cubs sat down to a delicious crawfish dinner. They ate every last critter in that bucket.

With dinners like that every night and plenty of rough wrestling, those panthers grew fast. By fall, they were ready to head out into the woods to fend for themselves. Sal bid them good-bye with a screech so loud and so high it broke the glasses in her mama's cupboards. It scared the panthers so bad they took off into the woods and never came back.

Without the cubs to care for, Sal had a little more time to herself. So she decided to collect some wildcat skins for her parents. Winter was coming, and she wanted her mama and papa to have nice cozy bedding to sleep in.

Sal was concentrating hard on one particular wildcat when a band of a hundred river ruffians snuck up on her. They circled her so fast that she couldn't get a proper screech out in time. And though she whirled and kicked and fought like the dickens, there were too many of them.

The ruffians wasted no time tying Sal up and carrying her off to their lair. The men smelled like rotten river water. Sal tried to ignore the foul smell as they moved deeper and deeper into the woods. When they arrived at the ruffians' filthy hideout, they tied Sal to a tree. Then the men set about building a roaring fire to keep warm through the night.

Soon the ruffians started to argue about what to do with Sal.

"I say we kill her right here and now," one of the men said.

"Naw, we got to use her to get that low-down, stinkin' Mink Fink," growled another. "She'll be mighty fine bait for his death trap."

"She'll fetch a high price on the auction block," another put in, eyeing Sal greedily.

The argument quickly turned into a shouting match. And then a fistfight. Sal watched from under a half-closed eyelid as the men yelled and wrestled and punched. Several slipped and fell on the garbage and food scraps that littered the ground.

The shouting got louder and louder as the men got angrier and angrier. Finally, the bandits were fighting so hard that Sal saw her chance.

"Hi-yi-yi-yo!" she bellowed. She broke free of her ropes as if they were nothing more than apron strings.

The ruffians stopped dead in their tracks and turned to the tree where Sal had been tied. She came flying off a branch feetfirst, knocking twenty of them into the fire. Kicking like a rodeo horse, she sent the rest of them into the flames as well.

"Yowww!" the bandits shouted as their skin crackled and sizzled. Racing out of the flames, they rushed to the river to soak their charred skin.

"Yi-pee-yi-yi-yo!" Sal shouted triumphantly. "Y'all needed a bath somethin' fierce!" She took off at a dead run through the woods, shouting all the way and waking folks all the way from Minnesota to the mouth of the Mississippi. And as for the ruffians, they never bothered Sal or her father ever again.

Stormalong
Superior Sailor

Alfred Bulltop Stormalong was first brought to life in a chantey called "Old Stormalong." Chanteys are songs that sailors sang while they worked on the great sailing ships of the late 1800s. In 1930, Frank Shay published some of the old stories and songs written about Stormalong — an invented character. Since then, the legendary sailor has grown several fathoms in popularity.

ALFRED BULLTOP STORMALONG, called Stormy for short, was deckhands down the best sailor that ever was. He lived when there were still plenty of clipper ships out on the high seas. In case you don't know much about ships, clipper ships were beautiful wooden boats with giant, billowing sails. They crossed the seas in the 1800s. These days you don't see many clipper ships, just ore boats and steamships and the like.

Nobody is quite sure where Stormy was born, but most folks believe it was in one of those old Massachusetts towns that ends in "tucket" or "port" or "mouth." The important thing, one could suppose, is that he was born right next to the ocean. Because that was just where Stormy belonged.

Stormy was not your average kid. For one thing, he was tall. By the time he was ten he measured two fathoms, which is twelve feet!

Being on land was pretty awkward for Stormy. He couldn't go to school with the other kids because he was too big to fit inside the schoolhouse. And his voice was so loud that whenever he spoke he knocked people down.

So Stormy spent most of his time at sea. His favorite pastime was swimming way out to wrestle with the sharks. Or riding sidesaddle on a blue whale until he got tossed into the air by a gush from its blowhole. Stormy spent so much time in the deep blue ocean that folks swore he had salt water in his veins instead of blood.

By the time he was twelve, Stormy had grown to three fathoms, a full eighteen feet! Stormy had now completely outgrown his township, so he decided to take to the sea for good. He dove into the ocean and swam a two-minute sprint to Boston. When he got there, he searched the harbor for the biggest ship he could find. The *Silver Maid* seemed to be the perfect one, and it was about to set sail for China.

"I'd like to hire aboard your ship," Stormy said to the captain.

The captain was almost blown off his feet by Stormy's big voice. If he hadn't been a sailor and used to giant waves sloshing over his deck, he certainly would have been knocked over. Instead, the captain steadied himself and pulled out his telescope so he could have a good look at Stormy.

"Well, blow me down," the captain said, dropping the telescope. "You're the biggest sailor-man I've ever seen in these parts."

"I'm not a sailor-man, but I aim to be," Stormy replied. "Right this minute I'm just a twelve-year-old boy. But I know the sea better than anything, and I'd like to make your ship my home for a spell."

"Twelve years old is just the right age for a cabin boy," the captain said, shielding his eyes and gazing up at Stormy. "And you sure look like you can handle the work. You're hired, son."

Stormy grinned and climbed aboard. But he was in such a hurry that he stepped too close to the rail and almost tipped the *Silver Maid* right over!

"Whoa there, little Stormy," the captain said. "Keep yourself in the center of the boat, and we'll cross the seas just fine."

Stormy followed the captain's advice and learned a few other things, too. Like he couldn't swab the decks too hard or the wood would just rub right off. And at night, when he went to sleep in the ship's biggest rowboat, Stormy had to be careful not to turn over. Whenever he did, giant waves pounded the *Silver Maid's* decks. More than once, the sailors practically drowned in their sleep from Stormy's tossing and turning.

As long as Stormy was very, very careful, things went along pretty well. The ship made it safely to China, where the captain traded furs for silks, spices, and tea. Then the *Silver Maid* turned around and headed home.

By now, all the men on board were crazy about Stormy — except maybe the cook. Stormy ate so much salt pork and so many ostrich eggs and loaves of bread that the cook never got any sleep. He had to run the galley thirty-two hours a day just to keep up with the cabin boy's appetite.

One day, the *Silver Maid* was zooming along at a hundred-fifty knots when it suddenly stopped short. The sailors were hurled forward, and some of them flew clear overboard. Quick as a flash, Stormy fished them back out like flies from a bowl of buttermilk.

The captain peered over the deck. His eyes grew wide as saucers. Only one thing could have brought the *Lady* to such a halt: a deep-sea creature so big and so horrifying that thoughts of it kept even the bravest sailors up all night. Something with multiple heads, arms, and a giant mouth.

"A kraken," the captain whispered.

Stormy had no idea what a kraken was. But he didn't care. "I'll take care of it," he declared. And before anyone could stop him, Stormy dove into the sea.

Down, down, down he swam, until he was underneath the big ship. The water was inky black, and Stormy could barely see. Suddenly, a giant tentacle grabbed him by the arm and dragged him forward.

The next thing Stormy knew, he was staring into the giant eyeball of the biggest, slimiest, most tentacled sea creature he'd ever seen or heard of. (Having spent his entire life in, next to, or on the sea, that was a *lot*.) The creature — indeed a kraken — had wrapped most of its forty tentacles around the keel of the *Silver Lady*. And now about a dozen more were wrapped around Stormy. Unfortunately, Stormy had leaped off the boat so quickly he didn't have any kind of weapon with him.

Stormy thought fast. Grabbing a tentacle, he twisted it up into the sailor's knot called a figure eight. Then, with another tentacle, he tied a half hitch. Then a cat's paw. And then a becket bend.

The kraken thrashed and tried to grab Stormy with one of its untied tentacles. It tried to get its giant mouth around Stormy's pinky. But even the terrible kraken was no match for the cabin boy. Stormy tied every one of those forty tentacles into all kinds of sailor's knots, and then made up more than a dozen knots of his own.

Above, the sea was churning so hard that the ship almost sank. The sailors clung to the rails for their lives.

Then, suddenly, everything went still. The ship began to move forward over the smooth sea. The sailors let go of the rails and waited for Stormy to resurface. They waited a long time. Finally, when they were about to give up, Stormy burst out of the water and climbed aboard.

The boat tipped sharply to the port side as he climbed in, and the sailors had to cling to the rails again. But nobody minded one bit.

"That baby kraken won't be bothering us anymore," Stormy announced.

The sailors whooped and hollered.

"Well, blow me down," the captain said gleefully. Then he held up his hands. "On second thought, don't!" Stormy laughed a mighty laugh.

When the *Silver Lady* landed back in Boston, Stormy bid good-bye to his sailor friends. Though he loved the sea and his friends, the *Silver Lady* was just too small for him. And he was still growing. He needed to find a place where he could really stretch out.

Folks disagree about where Stormy

headed next. Some say he joined John Paul Jones and helped him finish off the American Revolution. Others say he headed west on foot and became a potato farmer for a while. Only one thing is for sure. Years later, Stormy turned up on the shores of the Atlantic again. And this time he had a plan.

You see, Stormy loved the sea more than anything. The sea, after all, was plenty big for him. What wasn't big enough for him were the ships that sailed it. So he decided to build one for himself.

Stormy hired the best shipbuilders he could find — more than three thousand of them. They worked day and night for three years building Stormy's beautiful ship, which he named *Albatross*. The ship was so big that the sail tailors had to sew the sails out in the Sahara Desert, just so there would be room to lay them out. They used ten-foot-thick rope for thread.

The *Albatross* required so much wood

that there was a five-year lumber shortage after she was built. It took forty men just to steer her, or Stormy's entire pinky finger. But she was a beautiful ship, worthy of a captain like Alfred Bulltop Stormalong.

Finally, Stormy had a ship he could stretch out on. Of course, there were a few snags here and there. The *Albatross* was so big that its masts occasionally banged into the sun and moon. Stormy fixed that by padding them with hundreds of furs from the cargo hold. The masts were so tall that cabin boys who climbed up to the crow's nest came back down bearded old men. Stormy had to hire the fastest teams of white horses he could find to carry sailors from stem to stern. Even so, the trip often took three weeks because the horses had to stop to rest once in a while. And the ship was too big for any harbor, so the cargo had to be loaded onto regular-sized ships out at sea and transported to land.

But perhaps the biggest snag occurred when the *Albatross* was making a journey from the United States to England. Stormy was carrying an important shipment of fresh foods and was in a hurry to get to his destination. But when they got close to the English Channel, Stormy could see it wasn't wide enough.

"We're in a mite of trouble, boys," he yelled to his four hundred hands. "Bring up all the soap you can find below, and slather her sides good."

Some of the crew members thought Stormy had gone a little wacky in the head. But they did as they were told without complaint. They frothed up the sides of the *Albatross* as best they could.

Sure enough, when they got into the channel, the *Albatross* squeezed up tight against the black cliffs of Dover. For a minute it looked like she might bust up, but then she slid on through like an eel through a fisherman's hands. It wasn't until the sailors turned around that they saw that their lathered-up *Albatross* had turned the cliffs of Dover a pearly white. They're still white today, and the churning sea below is frothy with suds.

Stormy and his men happily sailed the seas for many years. They rolled over the sparkling blue waves with glee, feeling the salt air on their faces and in their beards. They transported cargo from Russia to the United States, Europe to China, and everywhere in between.

But sometime in the late 1800s, clipper ships began to be replaced by hulking steamships. These coal-burning vessels didn't need the wind to propel them, and the beautiful sight of clipper ships on the oceans began to disappear. The clipper ship captains seemed to disappear right along with them.

No one is sure where Stormy ended up. Rumor has it he died in a race against a steamship. Or perhaps he simply disappeared into the sea. But wherever he went, his spirit is still out there on the ocean, steering his giant *Albatross* with a single pinky finger.

Bess Call
Mountain Strongwoman

The Adirondack Mountains of New York State were home to strongman Joe Call and his sister, Bess. Newspapers and storytellers alike claimed that Joe was the strongest man in the entire United States, and no one dared disagree. Bess was nearly as strong as her brother, and a raven beauty to boot. She faced any strength-testing challenge that came her way with power and grace.

BESS CALL lived in New York, way up in the Adirondack Mountains. She shared her home with her brother, Joe, the strongest man in the United States. Joe was so strong that he could lift a steer with his little finger or pull trees right up out of the ground, roots and all. Bess could, too.

When Bess was born she weighed a mighty twenty-two pounds, and her eyes and skin were shiny black. Folks called her a real beauty.

But she was more than beautiful. Bess was strong — and even stronger-willed. Before she was two years old, Bess decided she didn't like her crib by the window, so she picked it up and moved it closer to the fire. Then she hauled in a wheelbarrowful of wood to get the flames crackling and roaring.

In spite of her size and strength, Bess's ma and pa tried to get her to act like a lady. But Bess paid them no mind. She was too busy roaming the woods, climbing trees, and rearranging those giant Adirondack boulders.

One afternoon, Bess was looking for something to do. She looked up at Pitchoff Mountain, which had a nice flat section on one side.

"I think I'll spruce that mountain up with something," she said to herself. So Bess carried a whole heap of boulders up Pitchoff Mountain and placed them on top of one another, creating a sculpture. Today folks call that place Balanced Rocks.

Bess used her strength to move more than boulders. Especially around her parents' farm. She did barn chores real efficientlike. She never bothered to move a horse or cow out of its stall when she was cleaning manure. She simply lifted the animal into the air with one hand and swept the stall with the other.

If she was shoeing horses, she'd hold 'em up in the air while she slapped the iron shoes onto the animal's hooves and pounded 'em on tight with nails.

When it was time to turn the compost pile, she didn't spend hours mixing it with a pitchfork, like regular folks. She just lifted the entire compost shack into the air and turned it over. A few days later she'd turn it back, so the rich fertilizer was mixed evenly, like a cake batter.

When Bess got to be school age, she trudged off with her brother to the one-room schoolhouse. Bess didn't care much for school, though she was smart as a whip. When she put her mind to it, she could finish her lessons faster than anyone else. But usually her mind was on something besides lessons. Like how many desks she could lift with two fingers (eleven, she discovered, when the teacher's back was turned).

During recess, Bess would keep herself busy rearranging trees and boulders while her brother prowled the playground looking for someone to tussle with. Joe liked to practice his wrestling. Though he always won, he was gentle and never broke more than a few of his opponents' bones. Everyone agreed he was a good sport.

As Joe got older, though, nobody in the county was a good enough match for him. A few folks still liked to wrestle Joe Call, but winning was too easy for him. There was no fun in it anymore — Joe needed more competition. So he set out into the world to find some worthy challengers.

Joe was gone a long time, and Bess missed her brother terribly. But she had her work cut out for her. You see, once in a while someone would want a good Adirondack tussle. With Joe out traveling, Bess was the obvious wrestling choice. She got so good that she could pin three men at once, using only her left hand.

Eventually, Joe got tired of traveling and wrestling and came back home. He and Bess bought some land and set about building a farm.

"I'll move those boulders out of the way so you can plow the earth," Bess told her brother one morning.

Joe nodded, and Bess ran across the field, picking up the giant rocks. She tossed them into the air like pebbles. They landed hard in the soil in the shape of a giant circle. That winter it snowed a lot, and when the spring thaw came it turned that circle of rocks into the shores of Heart Lake.

Together Bess and Joe farmed their land, growing the sweetest vegetables and richest grains. Folks from far and wide still came to call on Joe, looking to wrestle him. Joe was tired of wrestling, but sometimes these folks wouldn't take no for an answer.

"I've come all the way across the Atlantic Ocean," one man complained. "And

I'm not leavin' until you wrestle with me."
So Joe had no choice but to hold his plow
up in the air and pin the man in a hurry.
One match was enough for the man, then
he was quick to be on his way back across
the ocean.

It wasn't long after that that Joe went
into town to buy supplies for the farm.
While he was gone, Bess decided to give
the house a good scrub, and she got to
work in the kitchen. She was holding the
stove above her head and mopping underneath it when there was a knock on the
door.

Setting the stove down, Bess went to
see who had come calling. It was a
stranger, and right away Bess knew that he
had come to wrestle her brother. The
stranger's horse was tethered to the front
porch.

"Mornin', ma'am," the stranger said.
"I've come looking for Joe Call."

Bess opened the door with a sigh. "My

brother's not home," she said. "He's gone to town."

The stranger looked disappointed. "I've come clear across seven states to wrestle the famous Joe Call. Mind if I wait a while?"

"Suit yourself," Bess replied. "I'll just keep on cleanin' the kitchen."

The man went back out on the porch while Bess finished her work. Soon it was afternoon, then evening. Bess invited the stranger in for supper.

"Joe's bound to be mighty late," Bess said, washing down a hot biscuit with a gulp of fresh milk. "I usually do his wrestlin' when he's away. That be all right with you?"

The man blinked in surprise, then laughed. "You're a woman," he sputtered.

Bess tensed, and the tin milk cup in her hand crumpled. She got to her feet and glared down at the man. "You ready to wrestle?" she asked.

Before the man could reply, Bess grabbed him by the seat of his pants and tossed him into the yard. Then she stomped out after him, ready to give him the tussle of his life.

The stranger had barely dusted himself off when Bess came at him. They tussled and tassled, kicking up so much dust that folks thought a swarm of insects was coming. Bess tried to go easy on him, seeing as he had the long journey home in front of him.

Finally, she got bored. She'd had enough. Picking him up for a second time, she tossed him over the fence.

The stranger groaned as he got to his feet. Brushing the dust off his behind, he looked over the fence at Bess.

"If you wouldn't mind throwing me my horse," he said, "I'll be heading off, then."

"Happy to," Bess said with a chuckle. She untethered the man's horse. With a graceful swing of her arm, she tossed the animal over the fence. It landed on its four hooves and gave a soft whinny.

The stranger wasted no time in mounting his horse. He set off at a gallop, racing down the dusty Adirondack road.

After that, no stranger ever mocked an offer to wrestle Bess. In fact, few strangers had the courage to show up on the Calls' doorstep at all. Those who did were mighty brave but were always outdone when it came time to tussle with the mighty Bess Call.

John Henry
Steel-drivin' Man

Historians disagree about John Henry. Many believe he was a real man who worked for the railroads in the 1870s. Others think he was a legendary character brought to life in the hammer songs created by hardworking steel drivers. One thing is for certain. John Henry was so important to the steelworkers that by the early 1900s nearly a hundred hammer songs like the ones in this story had been created in his honor.

FOLKS near and far knew something special was happening when John Henry was born. The night was pitch-black. The southern air and the animals were completely still. Then a crow cawed, a dog barked, and the panthers in the forests screamed.

A giant black cloud came from the west to cover the red moon, and rain poured down. Lightning split the sky, and thunder roared behind it like a steam train. Some folks even say the thunder made itself into a hammer and pounded the ground until it shook like there'd been an earthquake.

That's when John Henry was born.

As soon as he was out of his mama's belly, the storm passed. The rain stopped, the sky cleared, and a fresh mountain breeze blew over the land.

People could see that John Henry was special. First off, he was big. He weighed more than forty pounds when he took his first breath. Second, he was strong. His skin was shiny black, and his arms and legs — which were as big as stovepipes — bulged and rippled with muscles. Third, he was born singing. The song was simple, and went like this:

> *Oh, my hammer,*
> *Hammer ring,*
> *While I sing,*
> *Oh, hear me sing!*

At first the people weren't sure what to make of him. Who ever heard of a baby boy born singing about a hammer? But when John Henry raised a hand, they understood. There, clutched in that baby's mighty fist, was a hammer with a shiny silver head. The child had been born with a hammer in his hand.

John Henry grew fast. You could say he ate his way right through childhood. For breakfast he'd eat two kettles full of black-eyed peas, half a dozen ham bones, and twenty mixing bowls of stewed cabbage with gravy. For lunch and dinner he'd eat even more.

Now, when John Henry was a boy, cotton growers in the South still had slaves. John Henry lived with his family on a large plantation. One good thing about that was that John Henry's parents didn't have to worry about keeping their boy fed — that was the plantation master's job.

When he wasn't eating or growing, John Henry was working in the fields. He could pick cotton five times faster than anybody else, and his cotton was cleaner — no stems or pods in it. Though his mama and papa were proud of him and loved him with all their hearts, John Henry had a longing in his heart. When the workday was done he'd practice swinging his hammer, listening for the sound of the railroad. The train whistle was music to John Henry's ears.

By the time John Henry was a teenager,

he was as big and strong as the biggest, strongest men on the plantation. Not long after that, the Civil War ended, and he became a free man. So John Henry kissed his mama and papa good-bye and headed north, where he had heard a company called the Chesapeake and Ohio — the C & O — was building a railroad.

Being as big and strong as he was, it took John Henry only a few days to cross several states on foot. He was in West Virginia lickety-split. There he heard the clanging sound of men driving steel spikes into rock.

"That's what I was born to do," John Henry said, swinging his own hammer in his hand. "I'm born to be a steel-driving man."

Soon John Henry spotted men in groups of three. They stood around a steel spike, which a fourth man held in place. The three men took turns pounding the spike into the rock with long, shining hammers. Once the steel drivers had pounded holes into the rock, other workers would fill the holes with explosive powders and blow the rock to kingdom come. They were digging the Big Bend Tunnel for the C & O Railroad.

John Henry felt the rhythm of the hammers pounding in his soul. He walked right up to the overseer, whose name was Captain Tommy.

"I want to drive steel for you, and I'll be good at it, too," he said.

Captain Tommy sized up John Henry. "I can see you're powerful enough," he finally said. "But it's mighty hard work. Have you driven steel before, son?"

John Henry shook his head no. For even though he knew in his heart he was a steel-driving man, he was no liar.

"Then I'm afraid I can't offer you a job," Captain Tommy said. "Steel driving takes practice and skill, and you might hit somebody when you swing your hammer."

"I won't hit anybody," John Henry said slowly, "because I can drive steel by myself."

Hearing this, a whole group of steel-driving men looked up. They scowled at John Henry. *Nobody* drove steel by themselves. It took three men and a shaker (the man who held the spike), and that was that.

Then, suddenly, one of the men started to laugh. Soon the whole group of steel drivers was yacking it up. John Henry stood proud and firm.

"I'm a steel-driving man, and I mean what I say," John Henry said.

"I'll hold the spike," one of the shakers said suddenly. His name was Little Bill. He picked up a steel spike and set it in the rock. The overseer had no choice but to give John Henry a chance.

John Henry walked over to the rock and Little Bill and got himself ready to swing the hammer. You'd think he would have been nervous, never having done it and with all those people watching. But John Henry was thinking about only one thing — getting that steel into the rock as far as he could.

John Henry looked at the steel spike. He felt the weight of the hammer in his hands. He got a feel of the rhythm that hammer would make — in his fingers, in his shoulders, in his legs and arms. And then, when he was ready, he swung.

This old hammer (wham!)
Rings like silver, (wham!)
Shines like gold, (wham!)
Shines like gold! (wham!)

John Henry drove that steel into the rock faster than any team of three men had ever done. Captain Tommy hired him on the spot. From then on, any team of steel-driving men was thrilled to have him working with them.

Finally, John Henry was happy. He was born to drive steel, and driving steel he was.

And around about this time John Henry found himself a good woman, whose name was Polly Ann. She was a steel driver in her own right, and helped John Henry from time to time. John Henry and Polly Ann got married and set up house together, and were happy as could be.

Every day, from morning to night, John Henry went to work hefting that hammer, never missing a single strike. He was the best steel driver in the world. He could pound a spike into any kind of rock there was, in any direction.

Most steel drivers used a single nine-pound hammer. Not John Henry. He used a twenty-pounder. He worked so fast that sometimes Little Bill, who always held his spikes, had trouble keeping up with him. They had to keep pails of water on hand in case John Henry's hammer handle caught on fire.

It was hot and dusty in the Big Bend Tunnel. So hot that sometimes smoke started coming out of the steel drivers' ears. So dusty that the workers had to bend over just to see the steel spikes they were pounding. But despite the hard conditions, John Henry was content. He loved driving steel, and he loved digging that Big Bend Tunnel.

Then, one day, a man drove right up to the work site. He was looking for Captain Tommy.

"I've got a machine that will dig your tunnel better than any crew of men," he boasted. "My steam drill will save you time and money."

Captain Tommy sized up the man. He was fond of his crew, and especially John Henry. He didn't want to see them out of work.

"I wouldn't be so sure about that," Captain Tommy replied, "because I've got a mighty fine crew, *and* John Henry. John Henry is the best steel driver in the world."

"No man is faster than this here machine," the man declared. "If John Henry can beat it, why, I'll give it to you for free."

Captain Tommy longed to take that bet. He wanted to put this bragging Yankee in his place. But he couldn't do it without John Henry's consent, so he called him over.

"This man says his machine can out-drill you, and I say it can't. How do you feel about a contest, John Henry?"

John Henry looked the Yankee in the eye. He looked at the machine. He felt his twenty-pound hammer in his hands. For the first time in his life, he felt afraid. Because he knew he would race the machine. And he knew that doing so might kill him.

"Before I let that machine beat me," he said, "I'll die with a hammer in my hands."

The men cheered, and the contest was set for the very next day. John Henry went home to talk things over with Polly Ann. She told him the contest was a bad idea, but John Henry was determined. So she fixed him a good supper and helped him shine his hammer head. Then the two of them got a good night's sleep.

Word of the contest spread as fast as John Henry's hammering. The next morning, crowds of people had gathered outside the Big Bend Tunnel. John Henry and Polly Ann had to squeeze through the crowd to get to John Henry's hammering place. He was on one side of the mouth of the tunnel, and the machine was on the other. Piles of sharpened drills of all different lengths lay in between.

"John Henry won't ever beat that steam drill," some of the people whispered.

"That steam drill won't ever beat John Henry," others declared.

John Henry wasn't listening to any of them. He looked over at the drilling giant and down at his hammer. "We're gonna do it," he whispered, stroking the handle. "Or die trying."

Captain Tommy raised a flag. The steam drill whistled, and the race was on.

John Henry brought that hammer down sure as anything, and the spike sank into the rock. But beside him the steam drill chugged away, and soon it had the lead.

John Henry started to sing, swinging his hammer harder with every verse. His muscles bulged and sweat poured off his shining body as that hammer came down again and again.

Before long, John Henry was almost even with the steam drill.

"Bring me another hammer," he bellowed. "It's time to really drive the steel."

With a hammer in each hand, John

Henry worked harder than ever. His heart beat to the rhythm of the clanging steel, and folks were sure the mountain was going to collapse at any moment. Soon John Henry had the lead, and the steam drill had to be shut down for repairs. But they'd only been hammering for three hours — there were still six to go.

Polly Ann watched anxiously from the sidelines. She was proud of John Henry, of course. But she was mighty worried, too.

The hours wore on. Little Bill replaced the steel spikes with longer and longer ones as the hole John Henry dug got deeper.

John Henry worked like lightning. White-hot sparks flew through the August air. Twice his hammers caught on fire.

There seemed to be a fire in John Henry's lungs, too. The roar of blood in his ears was deafening. His muscles strained and bulged as if they were about to explode. Still, he hammered on.

By the beginning of the ninth hour, John Henry was looking tired. But he kept on hammering as the sweat poured down his face.

"Time!" Captain Tommy called.

The crowd grew silent. The steam drill was shut down. John Henry slumped against the Big Bend Mountain and Polly Ann rushed to his side. Everyone waited for the measurements to be taken.

A few minutes later, the judges whispered something in Captain Tommy's ear. He turned to face the crowd.

"John Henry beat the steam drill by more than four feet!" he shouted.

The crowd cheered. The Yankee with the steel drill scowled. And John Henry fell to the ground with a mighty thud. Polly Ann cradled his head in her lap. "Oh, John Henry!" she sobbed.

Little Bill rushed up to John Henry, who was now staring up at the blue mountain sky. Captain Tommy was right behind him.

"You all right, John Henry?" Little Bill asked.

John Henry took a shuddering breath and gazed at the trees and the mountain overhead. "I beat the machine," he whispered. "And I'm dying with a hammer in my hand."

John Henry wrapped the strong fingers of one hand around Polly Ann's slender ones. His other hand held one of his hammer's handles. Then, with a final breath, he closed his eyes forever.

Annie Oakley
Sharpshooting Star

Annie Oakley was born Phoebe Ann Moses in 1860. By the time she was ten, she was hunting to help feed her family, and she killed a rabbit with her first shot. Annie honed her skills with a gun for years afterward and soon became the best shot in Ohio, and, later, possibly the world.

Annie performed in Buffalo Bill's Wild West Show and for Queen Victoria of England. She also beat the Grand Duke Michael of Russia in a shooting contest. Even though some people said she had, she didn't actually shoot a bullet all the way around the world (though maybe she could have if she tried!).

SOME FOLKS say that Annie Oakley was born with a rifle in her hands. Others insist that she didn't handle a gun until the ripe old age of two. But everyone agrees that she was the best sharpshooter the world has ever seen.

Annie was born in 1860 on the Ohio frontier. Back then, girls didn't shoot guns. They cooked and cleaned and sewed. They stayed home and tended house. But not Annie.

Annie loved the outdoors from the day she was born. And she loved hunting. She'd go searching for grouse and rabbits with her pa every chance she got and was soon his official bullet holder.

"That's an important job," he always told her, tousling her messy brown hair.

Annie grinned and watched carefully as her pa cleaned, loaded, and fired the gun. She loved the cracking sound of the gun going off.

When Annie was six, her pa up and

died. She was so sad that she cried for weeks on end. She loved her pa and their hunting adventures together. Who would she carry bullets for now?

It wasn't long before Annie decided she'd carry bullets for her own self. She'd carry a rifle, too. Her family was terribly poor with Pa gone, and terribly hungry, too.

"Someone's got to bring in fresh meat to keep us from starving," Annie declared as she started into the woods with her pa's rifle balanced on her shoulder. It was so heavy she could barely walk. But she trudged off just the same.

Annie spent every afternoon out in the Ohio woods and streams, hunting and practicing her shooting. She hunted and practiced and hunted and practiced. She always kept her gun clean. And she was very careful when she loaded it with gunpowder and lead bullets.

They say that when Annie looked through the barrel of a gun, a hush came over the forest. The wind stopped blowing. The leaves stopped rustling. Even the clouds in the sky stopped moving.

One thing was for certain. Annie never fired a gun until the moment was exactly right — until she knew she would hit her target. And she never shot a living thing unless she needed it for food or money. Back then, that was the way. Folks either shot their vittles or raised them in a garden.

Before long, Annie was bringing home so much fresh meat that her brothers and sisters had more than their fill at every meal. Between her game and what her ma grew in the garden, the family feasted on rabbit stew and thick soups and turkey and vegetables smothered in gravy.

"De-licious," her brother Johnny would declare. Johnny admired his older sister's talent with a gun. Sometimes Annie even allowed him to be her bullet holder.

By the time she was eight, Annie could shoot a whole school of fish out of an Ohio stream with a single bullet. Somehow those fish always ended up lying in a neat row on the riverbank, too. It was as if they were just waiting to be taken back to the farm so Annie's ma could fry them up for supper.

By the time she was ten, Annie could spin in circles until she was dizzy as a twirling top and still hit her mark. She could hang upside down from a tree branch, fire backward, and still shoot an entire flock of geese out of the sky. She could harvest *and* shell a pound of nuts from a tree with two shots. And some folks claim to have seen her fill up an entire bushel basket with wild berries that she shot clear off the brambles — *without* squishing any juice out of the fruit.

Since Annie only shot game clean

through the head, fancy restaurants wanted to buy her meat.

"That way," a restaurant owner named Jack Frost said, "my customers don't have to worry about biting into buckshot while they're enjoying a fine meal."

Annie's fur pelts were so popular that soon the rich and fashionable ladies in Cincinnati were wearing them to the ballet and the opera.

"Is that an Oakley?" one woman would ask another at intermission.

Pretty soon, word about Annie had spread far and wide. By the time she was fifteen she was known as the best sharpshooter in Ohio, and maybe the whole Midwest.

So it wasn't that surprising when the owner of the general store in town suggested that Annie participate in a shooting contest in Cincinnati. She'd square off against Frank Butler, a famous marksman. Frank was coming to town with his traveling shooting show and was offering to sharpshoot against anyone who had the guts. The winner would get a hundred dollars.

Annie had the guts, of course. But she thought it was a silly idea. Shooting had always been for survival, not for fun (even though she loved it more than anything). But the more Annie thought about it, the more she wanted to do it. She was excited about the challenge. Deep down inside she wanted to beat Frank Butler. Not to mention win a hundred dollars.

The day of the contest came. When the crowd of bristly men saw that Frank was competing against a fifteen-year-old sprite of a girl, they laughed out loud.

"I want my money back!" a few even said.

What kind of contest was that? they wondered.

Frank went first. A clay pigeon was hurled into the air, and Frank shot at it. A second after he did, the disk exploded. Annie went next, and her shot fired true. The pigeon became nothing more than a cloud of dust.

"A lucky shot," one of the men declared.

He was so surprised when Annie made her next shot that he almost bit his tongue clear off. (He was awful quiet for the rest of the match.)

Back and forth they shot. Over and over, each one hit the mark. Then, on his twenty-fifth shot, Frank missed. Annie didn't waste a second. She gave a little twirl, raised her rifle, and fired. The pigeon exploded into smithereens. Annie had won.

With that shot, Annie had won not just the match and a hundred dollars, either. She'd won Frank Butler's heart. He was so smitten with Annie that he instantly began to court her. He sent her romantic gifts of gunpowder and bullets, gun cleaners, and clay pigeons. A year later, the two were married.

Sometime after they were married, Annie and Frank went to see Buffalo Bill in Saint Louis, Missouri. Buffalo Bill ran the most famous western show there was — Buffalo Bill's Wild West Show.

Annie had been practicing a new kind of shooting and could shoot just about anything — an ash off a cigarette or a hole in a playing card. She demonstrated a few of these tricks to Buffalo Bill.

"I've heard about you, Missy," Buffalo Bill said. "And I'll be glad to have you in our show."

Folks came in hordes to see the petite Annie and her surefire tricks. She blew out candles with bullets. She shot tiny, whirling glass balls from the back of a galloping horse. She even shot specks of dust off Frank's fingers. Annie learned new tricks so fast that nobody knew what she was going to do next. They only knew she would never miss.

Buffalo Bill's show was so successful in the United States that they decided to go on tour in Europe. Annie and Frank went along. Their first stop was England, where they participated in Queen Victoria's Golden Jubilee — a giant party celebrating Victoria's fifty years as queen.

Queen Victoria was an active ruler, but she was rarely seen in public. Lots of folks said she wouldn't come to see the Wild West Show. Well, not only did the queen come, she demanded a second performance! And more than anything she wanted to meet the show's star, Annie Oakley.

Annie was a little bit nervous, but the queen was very nice. "You are a very clever girl," she told Annie.

Folks in England loved Annie as much as the folks back home did. Newspapers called her a shooting sensation. Fans sent her so many flowers that she had to dig her way out of her tent every morning with a shovel. One hundred and thirty-eight men sent letters proposing marriage. (Luckily, Frank was not the jealous type.)

Annie got other letters as well. One was a challenge from the Grand Duke Michael of Russia, who was visiting England. He fancied himself the best shot in the world and wanted a chance to beat Annie Oakley.

Bam! Bam! Bam! Bam! The grand duke was good and hit thirty-five of his fifty targets.

Annie lifted her gun and peered through the barrel. Bing! Bing! Bing! Bing! She hit forty-seven out of fifty. She was now officially the best shot in the entire world.

Annie won so many medals while she was in Europe that her trophy trunks barely fit in the cargo hold of the steamship back to America. Twenty thousand tons heavier, the vessel barely made it back across the Atlantic.

Old friends and fans in the United States welcomed Annie home with open arms. And she now had a new fan, too. He was Sitting Bull, the feared and respected Indian chief who had helped defeat General George Custer at the battle of Little Big Horn.

Lots of folks were afraid of Sitting Bull. They blamed him for the death of General Custer and many other soldiers. People booed and hissed him when he appeared in the Wild West Show.

Annie didn't give a hoot what people thought. She liked and respected Sitting Bull. He knew a lot about guns and weapons and even more about the outdoors. He was a great thinker. Sitting Bull called Annie Wan-tan-yeya Ci-sci-la, which means Little Sureshot. Annie called Sitting Bull a good friend.

One evening, Sitting Bull and Annie were talking together around a campfire.

"I have a challenge for you, Little Sureshot," Sitting Bull said. "You can shoot almost anything from almost any distance. But can you shoot something that is right next to you? Like this fence post, for instance?"

Annie looked at the fence post standing next to her. It was so close that she couldn't use her rifle. So there was no way she could shoot it. Or was there?

"I'd have to shoot a bullet all the way around the world!" she exclaimed.

Sitting Bull nodded and smiled. "Indeed you would, Little Sureshot," he said.

Annie thought the idea was crazy. But she had thought the same thing about squaring off against Frank Butler, too. And she always loved a challenge. . . .

Annie practiced for many weeks. First

she fired shots to the Southwest United States. Some of those shots lopped off the tops of mountains, creating the mesas. Next she aimed for Japan and hit Mount Fuji so hard it caused a volcanic eruption!

On the way through northern Europe, one of Annie's practice bullets created Norway's fjords.

Finally, Annie was ready to face her biggest challenge. By now, folks from near and far had heard about what she was going to try to do. They lined up for miles to see Annie's shot for themselves.

For the first time in her life, Annie felt a little nervous. But when she lifted her gun to her shoulder, everything went still. The crowd was silent. The wind stopped blowing. Annie thought only of the fence post next to her and pictured her bullet hitting it square in the middle.

Annie pulled the trigger. The bullet soared forward straight and true, then disappeared altogether.

The silent crowd waited. Annie held her breath. Frank Butler watched the sky anxiously. Only Sitting Bull seemed calm.

A minute went by, then two. Then fifteen. Exactly thirty-four minutes and eight seconds later, Annie's bullet pierced the fence post with an incredible thud.

"That is my Little Sureshot," Sitting Bull declared.

The crowd cheered. Frank Butler jumped up and down.

"Yahoo!" Annie shouted. She fired a bullet into the air.

Annie Oakley had met her biggest challenge ever . . . and made a few landmarks along the way.

Johnny Appleseed
Seed Sower

Johnny Appleseed was a real person. He was born John Chapman in Massachusetts in the late 1700s. When he was in his early twenties he began to travel westward, planting apple orchards and giving apple seeds to others, telling them to do the same. He wandered across the frontier for forty-eight years. Many of the most bountiful apple orchards in the Midwest are the result of his plantings.

APPLE PIE. Applesauce. Apple frit-
ters. Not to mention juicy, crisp apples
fresh off the tree. De-licious!

Hard as it is to believe, America might
not have any of these delectable delights if
it weren't for the tireless work of one man.
His name was Johnny Appleseed.

Johnny Appleseed was not a regular
tall-tale hero. He couldn't chop down several acres of trees with a single swipe of
his ax. He didn't ride on the back of an
alligator or wrestle giant sea creatures.
And he couldn't pound a steel spike into
rock faster than any man alive.

No, Johnny Appleseed was not that
kind of hero. He was a softer sort, the sort
who loved living things. He quietly made
his way through the woods, not disturbing
anyone or anything, and doing his very
important work.

Johnny Appleseed planted almost all
the apple trees from the East Coast to the
Ohio River valley, across Pennsylvania,

Ohio, Indiana, and Illinois. And he did it all traveling on foot!

The day Johnny Appleseed was born, a rainstorm pelted most of Massachusetts. It was springtime, and the skies opened up and let loose one of those earth-drenching downpours. Cats and dogs fell to the ground in heaps.

But when Johnny came out of his mother's womb, the skies cleared up and a giant rainbow spread clear across the state. One end of that rainbow landed right in Johnny's front yard. It got tangled in a giant apple tree that was so full of blossoms it looked like a giant snowball. Johnny stared at that apple tree for three days straight. It was the first sign that Johnny's life would have to do with apples. And did it ever!

As a child, Johnny spent all of his spare time in his parents' small apple orchard. In the springtime he'd climb into the trees and gaze at the apple blossoms, smelling their wonderful smell. In the summer he'd make sure the trees got plenty of water to drink. In the fall he'd pick each and every apple and make sure it was put to good use. In the winter he tested apple recipes.

After a while, Johnny's parents started to worry about him.

"You need to get out in the world," his mother told him. "There's more to life than apples. Why, there's animals and wildflowers and all kinds of things."

Johnny's mother took him out walking in the woods. Before long, he was almost as smitten with the wildflowers and shrubs and the animals as he was with apples. He'd spend all day out in the woods with the wild creatures until he heard his parents calling him in for supper. Then he'd head home, often cradling a lame squirrel or a wounded bird in his arms. He'd care for these creatures until they were well again, then he'd let them go.

Word spread about Johnny and his way with animals. Soon, folks from all over the county were bringing him sick creatures to care for. It's said that at one time Johnny was nursing five raccoons, four foxes, eight squirrels, a pair of motherless bear cubs, three skunks, nine possums, and an entire gaggle of geese.

Nobody is quite sure how Johnny managed to care for all these animals in addition to going to school, doing his farm chores, and tending the apple trees. What's even stranger is that all of the animals got along as if they were meant to be together under one roof. Soon they were all healed and back living in the wild, though they did come by to see Johnny from time to time.

One day, Johnny was sitting in the apple orchard munching on a crisp, ripe apple. He watched the covered wagons pass his family's farm, heading west. Folks were heading out into a brave new frontier in search of better futures. Life was just about perfect for Johnny, but those wagons got him thinking. Juice dribbled down his chin and he wiped it on his sleeve.

His head bobbed, and soon he was dreaming about apples . . . apples and apple trees spread out all over the new frontier. He pictured families planting apple seeds in the rich soil. He imagined them harvesting apples from the trees and eating them fresh, cooking them with meats, and baking them into delicious pies.

When Johnny woke up, he knew what he had to do. He would become an apple missionary. He'd plant apple orchards across the frontier, making sure that apples grew as far west as people journeyed.

Before long, folks heard what Johnny had a mind to do. Some of them thought he was a good and brave soul. Others simply laughed, calling him crazy. Johnny Appleseed didn't pay any attention to what people said. He simply put on travel clothes and headed west.

Johnny's first stop was the sweet-smelling cider presses of Pennsylvania. Cider was a pretty big business in Pennsylvania, and Johnny knew that once the sweet, juicy juice had been squeezed out of the apples, the squished apple pulp was thrown away.

"Mind if I take that leftover pulp?" he asked the mill owners.

"Not a bit," the owners replied. For to them, it was just garbage.

But not to Johnny. That pulp was full of something very important to his plan: apple seeds. He spent many weeks washing out millions of seeds and drying them in the Pennsylvania sunshine. Then he poured the seeds into small sacks made from whatever he could find — coffee sacks, flour sacks, or deerskin pouches.

Now, before Johnny could head farther

west, he needed some proper traveling clothes. So he pulled a nice big gunnysack from a pile of sacks and cut holes for his head and arms. Then he turned it upside down and slipped it on. He found an old tin pot and put it on his head for a hat. On his feet he wore nothing. Johnny liked to feel the earth under his bare soles almost as much as he liked apples.

Equipped with his new wardrobe, Johnny headed off. He traveled out of Pennsylvania into Ohio and then Indiana. Along the way, he planted as many seeds as he could in as many places he could — on hillsides, along riverbanks, and in grassy fields.

Johnny traveled day after day, week after week, season after season. He walked through sunshine, rain, sleet, and snow. He came across wild Indians and even wilder animals. But nothing ever hurt him, and he never hurt anything. In fact, he went out of his way to be kind to all living things. Animals in particular seemed to know this, and let him go freely about his business.

One time, Johnny was cooking a hot meal over a blazing campfire when a flock of giant, bird-sized mosquitoes flew into the flames. Many of the insects died. Horrified, Johnny put out the fire, declaring he'd rather eat a cold meal than cause another living creature's downfall. When he was finished eating his cold mush, he buried the insects in a mound of earth, along with a few shiny apple seeds. Today that site is the biggest apple orchard in Illinois.

Another time, Johnny was trying to escape a cold sleet and crawled into a hollow log.

"Grrrrrr," came a sound from the other end.

Johnny squinted and could just make out two round eyes in front of him.

"Excuse me, Mr. Bear," Johnny said politely as he crawled back out into the cold winter air. "I didn't realize this was your bed for the night." Back outside, Johnny curled up in a frozen snowbank and slept soundly the whole night through.

Johnny traveled far and wide, over mountains and streams and hillsides. He made it as far south as Tennessee and as far west as the base of the Rocky Mountains. He never got heatstroke or frostbite, or even too hot or too cold. He just loved being out in the woods, sowing his apple seeds in the rich soil.

When Johnny had too many seeds, he gave the extras to anybody who would take them — settlers, Indians, trappers, and boatmen.

"Plant these seeds in the good, brown earth," he told them. "You will soon have all the apples you could want — beautiful blossoms, sweet cider, fresh-baked pies, and spiced preserves."

Many people wanted to pay Johnny for

the seeds. Once in a while he would accept a meal or a place to sleep. But usually he simply told them that the apple trees would be payment enough.

"He's loony," some of the people said. But they were grateful for the shiny brown apple seeds just the same.

Years passed, and apple trees sprouted up all over the country. Their fragrant blossoms perfumed the air in the spring, and their boughs hung heavy with fruit in the fall.

By then, Johnny Appleseed's hair was gray and his beard was long and tangled. His gunnysack was in shreds, and the tin pot on his head was dented and scratched. But everywhere Johnny went, he saw people and animals enjoying the apple trees he had planted over the years. And that made Johnny happy.

Then one night, after a particularly long day's journey, Johnny sat down to rest in a small orchard somewhere in Indiana. It was springtime, and the air was sweet with the smell of apple blossoms.

As Johnny settled in for a good night's sleep, hundreds of wild animals gathered around him. There were bears and foxes and raccoons and possums. Squirrels and deer and birds and rabbits. They stood in a circle and watched Johnny Appleseed sleep peacefully. When Johnny woke up, he walked with them across the orchard and into a field, scattering apple seeds as he went.

In the morning, a traveler stopped in the orchard and came across Johnny Appleseed's cold, frail body. He still wore his gunnysack and the tin pot on his head. But strangely, his apple seed pouches were empty. Johnny Appleseed's work was finally done.

Look for all the
SCHOLASTIC JUNIOR CLASSICS